Goldilocks

and the Three Bears

retold and illustrated by

Tony Ross

Andersen Press • London

Once upon a time, not so very long ago, and not so very far away, there were three bears.

There was father bear, who was huge and gruff.

There was mother bear, who was middle sized and knew where the bandages and plasters were kept.

And. . .

. . . there was little bitsy baby bear, who was always getting into trouble, and getting lost, and getting his knees scratched.

The three bears lived together in a house which stood in a forest clearing.
They liked living there. They had lots to eat and a colour television set.
Life was good for the three bears. It was peaceful, and not much happened until the dreadful day when. . .

. . . Goldilocks got lost in the forest.

Goldilocks lived on the edge of the forest. Her dad was a forester, who cut up trees and cleaned up the forest after picnickers.

Goldilocks was playing as usual, but this time her games took her deeper and deeper in amongst the trees.

"Look out, Goldilocks," warned the rabbits. "You'll get lost!"

But Goldilocks took no notice. She didn't understand the rabbits' squeaks anyway.

As the sky grew darker, Goldilocks began to feel hungry and a little frightened. She stumbled round and round in circles, looking for the path home. But in the twilight, all the bushes and trees looked alike. The little girl was very, very lost.

Then she saw the house where the three bears lived.

Cautiously she crept up the path and rang the door-bell.

No-one answered, so Goldilocks gave the door a push. It swung open. "HULLOOOOOOOO?" she called. There was no reply.

The lights were on, but the house seemed empty.

Goldilocks was a rather nosey little girl, so she stepped into the hall
and peeped round a door into a lighted room. It was a dining room.
In the middle was a table set with three bowls.
Tiptoeing into the room, Goldilocks peered into the bowls.
They were filled with *porridge!*
"Hmmmmmm," thought Goldilocks. "That looks good!"
By now she was so hungry that her tummy was rumbling. So she took a
spoon and dipped it into the largest bowl.
"Yuk!" Goldilocks dropped the spoon. The porridge was *so hot!*

Wagging her tongue to cool it down, Goldilocks reached her spoon over to the middle-sized bowl and she took a mouthful of porridge. "Yeuhhhh!"

The porridge in the middle sized bowl was even worse.

It was *stone cold!*

"Who can live in this house?" thought Goldilocks. "And eat such *horrible* porridge?"

Goldilocks dipped her spoon into the last, and smallest, bowl and tasted the porridge, expecting it to be as awful as the porridge in the other two bowls.

But it was *just right*. It was *lovely!*

So, she took another spoonful, and another, and another...

In no time at all, the smallest bowl was empty.

Goldilocks licked the spoon, and her fingers.

She felt much better now, so she set off to explore the house.

The room next to the dining room was the sitting room. "What a good idea," thought Goldilocks. "I'll have a little rest!"

She was full of porridge, so she flopped down in the largest armchair. But it wasn't very comfortable, because it was *so big*. Goldilocks could only just reach the arms! She wriggled about for a moment and then decided to try another chair.

Climbing into the middle-sized armchair, Goldilocks tried to get comfy. First she sat *this* way, then she sat *that* way, but whichever way she sat, she couldn't get away from a big lump in the cushion.

"I wouldn't like to live here," thought Goldilocks. "The chairs are as bad as the food!"

Climbing off the middle sized chair, she looked around the sitting room.

There *was* another chair, a little bitsy one, in the corner.

Goldilocks sat in the little bitsy chair. It was *just right*.

Feeling pleasantly full of porridge, and rather sleepy, the little girl settled back for a snooze.

She had just closed her eyes, when... CRACK! SNAP! BONK!

Two of the little bitsy chair's legs broke. Goldilocks rolled onto the floor. Rubbing herself ruefully, she stared at the broken chair.

"Not a very good house, this!" she muttered. "I wonder if they've got any beds."

Feeling sleepy and bruised, Goldilocks wandered away to look.

Climbing the stairs, Goldilocks saw three doors. She opened the first one and found it was the bathroom, so she shut it.

Opening the second door, she saw a pleasant bedroom with two beds. Goldilocks jumped on the first bed, the *big* one.

"OUCH!"

It was so *hard.*

"Oh dear," she thought. "I'm *never* going to get a rest!"

Dispiritedly she slid off the shiny eiderdown.

The middle sized bed looked *much* comfier.

Goldilocks pressed the mattress. It felt soft enough.

Climbing onto the middle sized bed, Goldilocks sank into the sheets, and sank, and sank, *and sank.*

The bed was *too soft.* It was like drowning in a rag-bag.

Spluttering as she climbed out, Goldilocks scratched her head.

"There was a tiny bowl, and a tiny chair," she pondered. "Maybe there's a tiny bed!"

Remembering the third door, she hurried out of the big bedroom.

Pushing open the third door, Goldilocks found herself in a cosy little bedroom. In one corner stood a little bitsy bed.

She jumped on to the little bed, and shot up in the air.

The mattress was *so springy!* The little bed was *just right!*

Happily, Goldilocks snuggled under the blankets and fell asleep.

She was so tired that she forgot to take her shoes off.

While Goldilocks slept, the three bears arrived home.

They had been visiting great-aunt May, the old bear.

It was cold and dark, and the three bears were happy to be home.

"Don't know why we visit great-aunt May," grumbled father bear.

"She can't hear a word we say, and she just sits there knitting!"

"Never mind dear," soothed mother bear. "She never liked you anyway. Come and have your porridge."

She helped father bear off with his coat. Then all three trooped into the dining room. "Thought we shut the door," grumbled father bear.

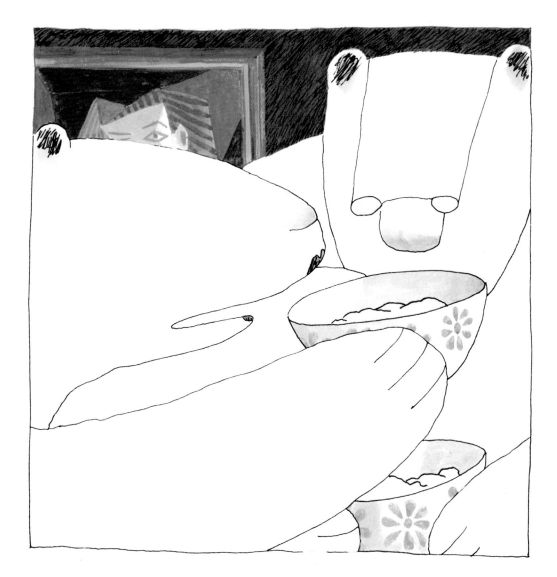

Mother bear sat father bear down at the table. He stared mournfully at his bowl. He knew something was wrong. He looked at the big bowl from this side and that, turned it round and hung his nose in it. Then he glared at mother bear.

"SOMEONE'S BEEN EATING MY PORRIDGE!" he roared.

Mother bear looked into the bowl for some moments. Then she looked into her bowl, the middle sized one.

"Someone's been eating MY porridge too!" she gasped. The two bears sat staring at each other, not knowing what to make of it.

Then baby bear looked into his little bitsy bowl.

"And someone's been eating my porridge too," he wailed, "AND EATEN IT ALL UP."

Baby Bear began to cry. Father bear got up and peered into the little bowl.

"Hmmmmm," he said, not knowing what else to say.

"There, there," said mother bear, drying baby bear's eyes for him.

"Better have a sit down, and think about this!" growled father bear.

"Thought we'd shut this door," said father bear, as the three bears entered the sitting room.

He took his paper, but stood glaring at his big chair.

"SOMEONE'S BEEN SITTING IN MY CHAIR!" he roared. The cushion was all rumpled.

Mother bear hurried over to her middle sized chair.

"Someone's been sitting in MY chair too," she said in wonder.

Father bear and mother bear stood scratching their heads and looking at their chairs. "Very *odd!*" grumbled father bear.

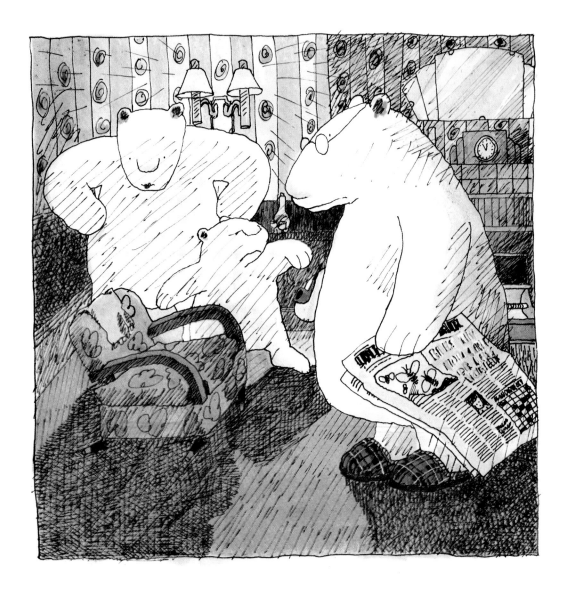

Then there came a long wail from baby bear.
"And someone's been sitting in MY chair and BROKEN it!"
Baby bear began to cry again.
Mother bear and father bear glared at the broken chair.
"I don't know what to make of it!" grumbled father bear. "There,
there," said mother bear, patting baby bear's head and drying his eyes.
"Let's go to bed," muttered father bear, "and think it over tomorrow."
The three bewildered bears plodded mournfully up the stairs
to their bedrooms.

Father bear pulled his pyjamas from under his pillow, but before he could put them on, he noticed the creased eiderdown.

"SOMEONE'S BEEN SLEEPING IN MY BED!" he bellowed.

Mother bear stopped looking for her curlers and went over to the middle sized bed.

"And someone's been sleeping in MY bed too," she said.

Just then, there was a squeal from baby bear's room, and father bear and mother bear rushed to see what the matter was.

Baby bear was standing by the open door of his room.

He was pointing with a shaky paw.

"SOMEONE'S BEEN SLEEPING IN MY BED TOO," he screeched,
"AND LOOK, SHE'S STILL THERE!"

The three bears gaped at Goldilocks, lying tucked up in baby bear's bed.

"Who is she?" whispered baby bear.

"Don't know," answered mother bear.

"Whoever she is, she should be in HER house, not OURS," grumbled
father bear.

The three bears knew now who had helped herself to their porridge, and who had sat in their chairs.

They were very ANGRY.

They stretched out their claws, and looked as fierce as they could (which was quite fierce, although not as fierce as the bears in the zoo).

Then, taking a deep breath, they went: "GRRRRRRRRRRRRR!"

Goldilocks sat up with a jolt.

She was so frightened, her hair stood up on end.

Goldilocks leapt out of the little bitsy bed, dived between father bear's legs, and bounded down the stairs, along the hall and out of the house. In her fright, she ran, and ran, and ran through the morning light! She soon found her way home, and she arrived puffing and red faced. Her dad was worried and angry at her being lost for so long, but Goldilocks had *really* learned her lesson.

From that day to this, she has *never* tasted anybody's food, or sat in anybody's chair, or slept in anybody's bed, or pried in anybody's house. . . without asking first!